# MUMSI Meets a LION

**Kim Stegall**

Illustrated by

**Kimberly Batti**

JOURNEYFORTH

Greenville, South Carolina

**Mumsi Meets a Lion**

Written by Kim Stegall
Illustrated by Kimberly Batti

Designed by Kelley Moore


Greenville, SC 29614
JourneyForth Books is a division of BJU Press

Printed in the United States of America


ISBN 978-1-59166-871-8

15 14 13 12 11 10 9 8 7 6 5 4 3 2 1

To Sawaya,
my Samburu friend,
who inspired this story
and to
Jeff, Margaret, and Cole,
who encouraged me to tell it
—KS

To my supportive family
and relatives
who continually inspire
my creativity
—KB

High in the mountains of Kenya lived a Samburu boy named Mumsi. Like the other boys of his tribe, he had learned many things about the ways of his remote village.

He knew how to hunt and herd and how to build a fire. He knew where to find the best toothbrush sticks to chew on all day to clean his teeth. He knew how to use his feet to mix mud for plastering on the low mushroom-shaped houses made by the village mamas.

Most importantly, he knew what to do if he ever came face to face with . . .

. . . a lion.

He had heard his parents tell him many times.

He had heard the mamas at the river. He had heard his father and the other babas in their meetings.

"If you ever come face to face with a simba," they would say, "look him straight in the eyes. Your eyes into his. Don't move; don't breathe. And whatever you do, don't run."

"The simba is a proud hunter. He wants to chase and catch his prey; he does not want things to be too easy. That is why the lion walks in circles, snapping sticks and purring low. He wants you to flee. And that is why you must stay still and never run from him. No matter what."

All the children listened closely at first. They whispered among themselves about what they would do if they ever met a lion.

They practiced a plan by choosing one to play the lion's part. The child-simba would snap twigs and make a rumbling deep in the throat. The other children always ran, shrieking and laughing at the silly game.

Only Mumsi stood stone still. It was as if a voice in his head were saying, *Don't move; don't breathe. And whatever you do, don't run.*

Soon the children forgot about the warnings. They went back to wrestling, shooting bows and arrows, and playing hide-and-seek. No one had seen a simba near their village for many years.

On the plains below the mountain, from a distance, they might catch a glimpse of a pride of lions—father, mother, and children.

But never up close.

Never anything to worry about.

One day Mumsi's mother and father sent him on an errand over the mountain to a neighboring village. "We need more tea," they told him. "We will need the chai for tomorrow's meal."

"Take your flashlight and spear!" Mumsi's mother reminded him as she tied to his belt a woven sack full of bright glass beads for trade. "You never know what might happen on your journey. Hurry there and hurry back."

So Mumsi ran. He reached the next village before the sun was high and hot. It had taken him much of the morning on a steep path that wound through thick forest.

He traded the beads his mother had given him for chai and filled the sack with the tea leaves. Warm chai would taste good with tomorrow's meal of boiled vegetables and his mother's chewy round bread.

Pleased with his good trade and not a bit tired, Mumsi started back over the mountain along the same path he had taken earlier.

This time he paused to pick the dark, sweet berries that grew in the forest. He ate until they stained his lips and tongue purple.

A little way off the path he saw a colony of dwarf mongooses the color of overripe tomatoes.

Mumsi stopped to watch them scamper in and out of an abandoned termite mound.

He did not notice that at his back the sun had begun to set.

Lengthening shadows made Mumsi grab his flashlight and spear and head back to the path. He did not worry because he knew that he had enough time to return to the village before the night grew completely black.

He clicked on his flashlight to see better in the darkening forest, and he held his spear firmly at his side. The sun had set behind the trees, and only the flashlight lit the forest now.

Mumsi knew that his parents would soon look for him. They had told him to hurry.

Night creatures *skreaked* and *yowled* around him, and Mumsi grew weary of walking.

Somehow the path seemed longer than it had this morning.

He wished that he had started back earlier and that he had not stopped along the way and that he could rest just for a moment. . . .

Mumsi did not know how long he had slept in the soft grass beside the path when a roaring *thrum-thrumming* made him cover his head with his arms.

Above him the wing-*whoosh* of hundreds of giant bats filled the air, their wings spread as wide as he was tall.

He told himself that the mapopo would not harm him, that they were hungry only for ripe fruit.

But the thunderous noise had spooked him, and he jumped up and ran quickly along the path, leaving the bats to their midnight feast.

Mumsi had just reached the top of the mountain when he heard a loud hissing. *S-s-s-s-s-s-s-s.*

He stopped to listen. *S-s-s-s-s-s-s-s.*

There it was again. *S-s-s-s-s-s-s-s.*

Although he could see nothing yet, Mumsi knew what the sound meant.

A joka was nearby, probably hiding in the underbrush. Mumsi pointed his flashlight toward the noise.

From under a rock peered a black and gray snake. Its head was the size of Mumsi's fist.

Too late Mumsi realized that he must have stepped near the snake's den.

He had seen an angry joka attack a man before, and this snake was fat with fury.

Just as Mumsi raised his spear to defend himself, the joka shot from its hiding place and sunk long fangs into a green lizard near his feet.

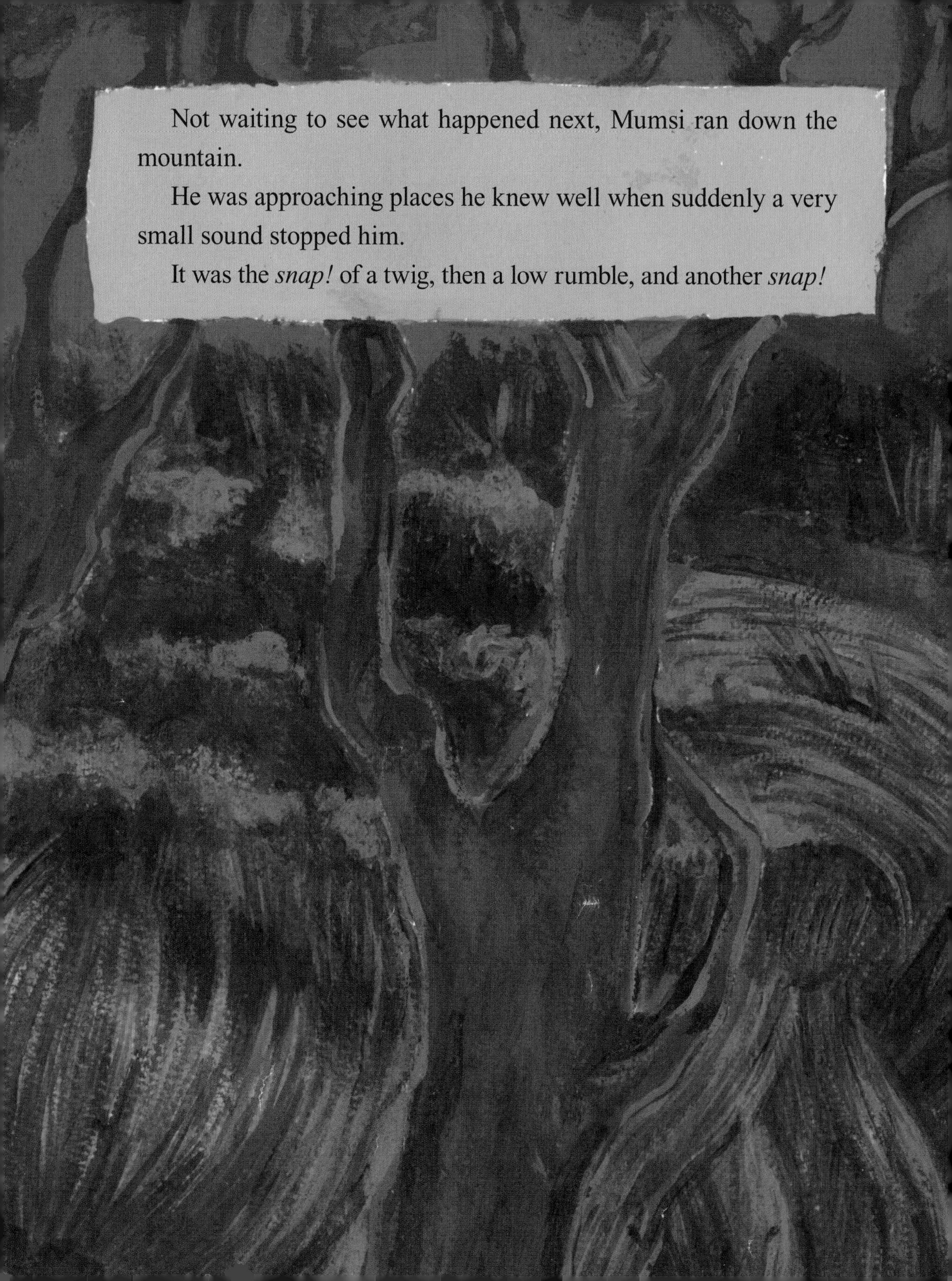

Not waiting to see what happened next, Mumsi ran down the mountain.

He was approaching places he knew well when suddenly a very small sound stopped him.

It was the *snap!* of a twig, then a low rumble, and another *snap!*

Bats and snake were almost forgotten as from deep in the forest appeared a great lion.

The simba stood across Mumsi's path almost close enough to touch. The flashlight's beam made a halo of the tawny gold mane.

The lion seemed to dare Mumsi to flee.

Mumsi thought quickly.

He had run from the mapopo.

He had run from the joka.

Then he remembered the voices he had heard so often.

*Don't move; don't breathe. And whatever happens, don't run.*

So Mumsi stood stone still.

He did not move. He barely breathed. And he did not run.

He stared at the simba in front of him, straight into glowing amber eyes ringed with black.

Eager for a chase, the lion stared back at Mumsi and flicked its tufted tail.

Mumsi knew that the lion was waiting to see who would move first and that he must somehow stay perfectly still.

No matter how tired or how afraid.

No matter what.

Sweat began to trickle down Mumsi's back. His legs ached to race toward home. The bag of chai felt like a heavy stone tied to his belt.

He thought about flinching, about throwing the spear. But he remained motionless.

He thought of counting the hairs of the simba's wiry mane. "Moja, mbili, tatu . . ." But they were too many and too close together.

A throbbing rumble let Mumsi know that the lion was still watching and waiting.

Just when Mumsi felt that he could keep still no longer, the light from his flashlight began to quiver and grow faint.

The next instant a deep darkness fell upon the forest.

The lion let out a long, low moan that seemed to shake the earth beneath Mumsi's feet.

As Mumsi braced himself for a pounce, over the mountain appeared the morning star, large and full of promise, silvering the sky and the trees and the two forest statues staring at each other.

In that shining moment Mumsi remembered one more thing that his parents had told him—lions hunt best in darkness.

Mumsi knew then that he would outlast the simba.

Minutes later a fiery orange sun rose; and the lion, weary of the standoff, stalked away.

For a long while Mumsi's feet stuck to the ground. He listened to the early morning forest chirp and buzz, click and trill.

He tried to breathe slowly, *in-out*, *in-out*.

When he had heard no lion sounds for many long breaths, Mumsi took a single stiff step.

Before he took another, he watched a bird with a long, curved beak eat a breakfast of beetles. Still there was no sign of the simba, and Mumsi was sure that the lion had returned to the pride.

He ran *chap-chap* down the path not stopping until he reached the edge of his village.

There he met his father and mother and other villagers coming toward him. They greeted him warmly, thankful for his safe return and glad to see his sackful of chai.

"Mumsi, you have done well," said his father. "Trading is difficult work. But what has kept you all night in the forest?"

So Mumsi began his tale about the playful mongooses that had delayed him, the flying mapopo and the hissing joka that had frightened him.

Then he told of the great simba. He could still see in his mind the black lips and glinting teeth of the lion that had stood across his path.

He looked at the village children who had gathered. "If you ever come face to face with a simba," Mumsi warned them, "don't move; don't breathe. And whatever you do, don't run."

"No matter what, Mumsi?" the children asked together.

"No matter what."